IF I Were A Superhero

Written by Serina B. Harris

Illustrated by Tiffany Baltimore

For Elijah and Elan

You two inspire me so much; my miniature heroes. I love you!

Your Mom,

Serina

"Pow, pow, vroom!" Danny exclaimed as he held his favorite action figure, Bullet, flying him through the air as the warm spring breeze flowed over his skin. Bullet was known for his lightning speed and a body harder than steel, which is how he earned his name. Danny loved action figures because of their special abilities like, flying, being invisible, and spitting fire. As he looked at Bullet and feeling the brown crunchy leaves beneath him, Danny began to think how amazing it would be if he were a superhero.

"If I were a superhero what would be my superpower?"

Mind reading was the first power that came to Danny's thoughts. With the power of mind reading, no one would be able to keep secrets from him. He could easily read his parents' thoughts and he would always know what his birthday gifts would be, even before opening them.

Danny's excitement grew because he would also know most of the correct answers on all his tests by focusing on the smartest kid in class during the quiz. But then he wondered, "Would I really want to know what everyone was thinking?"

The thoughts of others may be too loud; with all the sounds coming in all at once. It would cause all kinds of clutter and confusion, which would hinder him from hearing his own thoughts. Danny soon began to see himself with a headache, holding his hands over his ears trying to keep out the noise. So, he thought mind reading wouldn't be such a great superpower after all.

Danny looked over to the other side of the yard and spotted Misty, his little sister, running and playing with their dog Pippen. Danny believed Misty was smart for her age and she may have a good idea of an incredible superpower.

"Misty!" Danny yelled as he ran towards his sister and Pippen. "If you could choose any superpower in the world, what would you choose?"

Misty looked up at Danny as she wrapped her arms around Pippen's neck. Her lips twisted to the side as she thought long and hard before answering. "Hmmmm, I would fly!"

"Fly?" Danny replied. "What's so special about flying?"

"If I could fly I would go anywhere in the world, like the pretty beach we visited last year in Miami. I would fly over the beautiful blue water and feel the cool breeze in my face. Pippen would be my helper, so he would be able to fly too," she said with a smile as she hugged their furry friend.

Danny guessed if the entire family could fly they would be in the way of airplanes and maybe get knocked out of the sky by one of them.

Also, a family with a dog flying in the air would be such a distraction…the pilot can possibly crash, causing people to get hurt. Danny wanted to help others, not harm them. Flying seemed too dangerous. He decided it wasn't his choice as the perfect superpower. Danny turned around with his head down, feeling defeated.

"Thanks Misty, but I have to come up with something else," he stated as he made his way towards the front door. He then spotted his friend, Rob riding his bike in his direction.

"Hey Rob!" Danny yelled running towards Rob with his hand up. "I want to ask you something!"

"OK." Rob replied as he stopped riding and placed both feet on the ground to balance himself.

"What is it?" Rob continued.

"I've been trying to come up with the best superpower in the world and I can't think of anything. So, if you could choose any superpower, what would you choose?"

"Well," replied Rob. "I would choose light speed. With light speed, I could run and ride my bike faster than anyone on earth! I would play all kinds of sports like football and run track! I watch track and field with my dad and I really want to run against other people from other countries. Being the fastest boy, I'll win all the gold medals and everyone will know my name!" Rob stated in excitement.

He then hopped back on his bike and rode down the street as fast as his legs could carry him, making swooshing noises with his mouth.

As he turned the wheel on his bike to return to Danny, he nearly lost control by slipping on a small rock. Luckily, he quickly regained control of his bike with a quick change in position.

As Rob was riding back towards him, Danny thought light speed was a cool superpower, but he couldn't choose the same power as Rob. He had to be different.

"Thanks Rob." Danny said. "That's a cool superpower." Danny waved bye and went inside where Mom was reading her travel magazine in the family room. She looked so relaxed with her legs crossed and a small grin on her face as she flipped through the pages. He didn't want to disturb her, but he really wanted to know what Mom's superpower would be. Danny decided to wait until she was finished.

He picked at his fingers and stared at the stain on the carpet, that Misty caused drinking juice in the living room; he even hummed a little. As he waited, he continued to think about choosing the perfect superpower for himself. Sometimes Mom needs help getting the jelly jars opened. One time when they were moving into their new house, Daddy did most of the heavy lifting alone and he was exhausted.

Then suddenly it was as though a light switch went off in Danny's mind! Finally, he came up with the perfect superpower...super strength!

If he had super strength he would be able to lift cars, push through walls, and wrestle with lions. He would be the strongest boy on the planet and everyone would need his help, even Dad. Danny was so thrilled that he thought of a superpower useful for helping others that he loudly exclaimed.

"Mom, I've been trying to think of the perfect superpower for a super hero and I finally have one!"

"Really, what is it?" Mom asked looking away from her magazine with one eyebrow lifted.

"I would have super strength, so that I could lift the heaviest things with ease. I could lift cars when they break down on the road, push elephants out of the mud when they get stuck, just name it and I could move it!" Danny said as he tried to push the large gray chair Mom was sitting on.

"Wow, that's definitely super strength. So, would you be called a superhero only because you have super strength?" Mom asked.

Danny was confused and answered, "Well yes, all superheroes have an ability that makes them different from others."

"Do you think you can be a superhero without having super strength?" Mom asked.

"No, how can I be a superhero without powers?" Danny asked.

"Well, I'm sure you remember the time when the stray dog came after Misty."

"Yeah, how can I forget that?" Danny answered with a sigh. "I held the bike between the dog and Misty. I was so scared."

"Instead of running away you helped her and kept the dog back until help arrived." Mom said proudly.

"Yeah, I did, all the heroes I see on T.V. are brave." Danny said, straightening his shoulders and holding his head up high.

"You're my courageous son."

"Sometimes you even help Misty with her homework. Dad and I know that you're very bright. I've lived for quite some time now and with all the information I know about heroes, heroes are smart."

"Ok, but I do those things for Misty because she's my little sister and I don't want anything bad to happen to her."

"Danny, you do an amazing job taking care of Misty and showing her kindness; which reminds me of the day she fell out of the swing. She scraped her knee and began crying. You quickly rushed to her side." Mom said.

"Yeah, I dusted her off and helped her to her feet." he replied with a nod.

"You made her think that everything was ok."

"I was only being a big brother."

"Yes, but you were being a caring and loving big brother." Mom said with a big smile.

"Heroes are caring and loving too!" Danny exclaimed.

Danny began to think of all his skills and talents. Everything Mom said was true. He had done all those things for his sister, he even walks her to school in the morning. Sometimes he helps Rob with his chores so he that he has more time to play.

"Mom, you're right! I'm all that you say I am; caring, loving, brave, and smart. At first, I thought I was just being a nice brother and a good friend. I guess I can say if I were a superhero, I'd be a big brother!"

www.ingramcontent.com/pod-product-compliance
Lightning Source LLC
Chambersburg PA
CBHW041611120626
46551CB00002B/400